THE LITTLEST

Angel

To Rebekah, Anna, Nate, and Daniel
for being our examples of Christlike friendship
—Brooklyn & Hailey

Text © 2019 Brooklyn Parks & Hailey Bischoff
Illustrations © 2019 Brooklyn Parks
All rights reserved.

This is not an official publication of The Church of Jesus Christ of Latter-day Saints. The opinions and views expressed herein belong solely to the author and do not necessarily represent the opinions or views of Cedar Fort, Inc. Permission for the use of sources, graphics, and photos is also solely the responsibility of the author.

ISBN 13: 978-1-4621-2316-2

Published by CFI, an imprint of Cedar Fort, Inc.
2373 W. 700 S., Springville, UT 84663
Distributed by Cedar Fort, Inc., www.cedarfort.com

Library of Congress Control Number: 2018962227

Cover design and typesetting by Shawnda T. Craig
Cover design © 2019 Cedar Fort, Inc.
Edited by Kaitlin Barwick

Printed in the United States of America

10 9 8 7 6 5 4 3 2 1

Printed on acid-free paper

THE LITTLEST
Angel

- Written and Illustrated by -
BROOKLYN PARKS

- Cowritten by -
HAILEY BISCHOFF

CFI • AN IMPRINT OF CEDAR FORT, INC. • SPRINGVILLE, UTAH

In heaven,
everyone is bright.
Each person has a name.
We are all
very important.
No one is quite
the same.

We each have jobs.
We do our part
to do our Father's will.
You know our
Oldest Brother's here.
He has the
greatest skill.

But I? I am the
Littlest—they tell me
I'm so small.

I have no job,
I'm not so great,
and can't do
much at all.

"I have a noble task for you,"
said Father with a beam.
"Surely not me?"
What could I do? I couldn't even dream.

"Oh, yes, my Littlest Daughter,
a great big job for thee.
Find my Son. He will need a friend,
I think we can agree."

And so I drifted down to Earth.
The journey wasn't far.
I made my way to Bethlehem
beneath the shining star.

And there I found the little Prince
beside His mother dear.
He was so bright and innocent.
His light so very clear.

We gave each other timid looks,
and then I knew right there
that only He could see me now
so I could show my care.

We spent many days together,
ever in Father's sight.
We learned lessons of the Spirit
like butterflies of light.

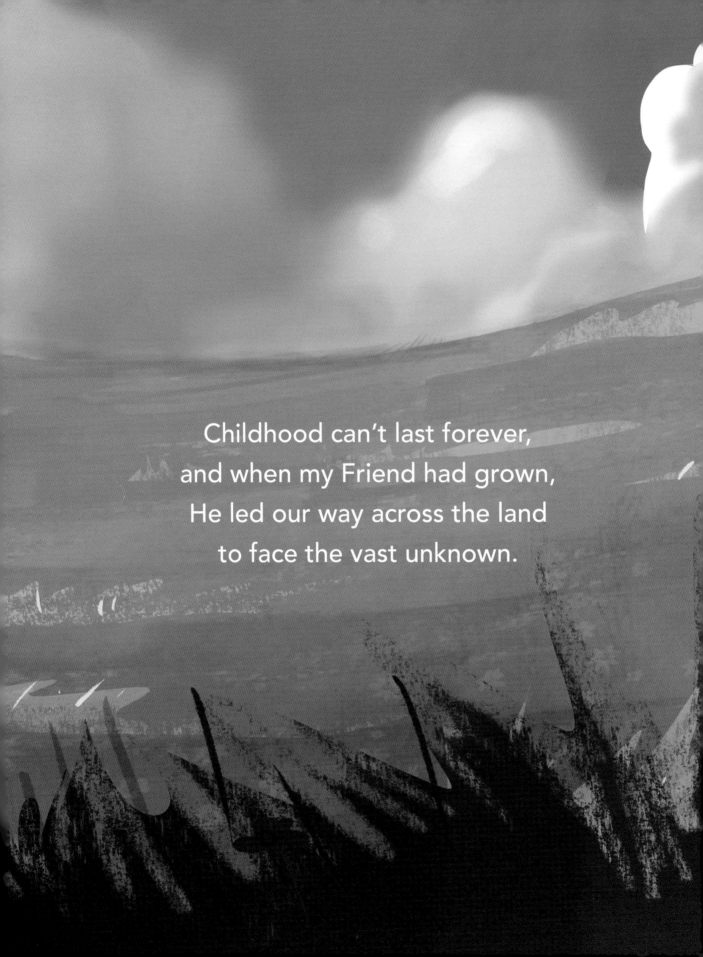

Childhood can't last forever,
and when my Friend had grown,
He led our way across the land
to face the vast unknown.

By listening to Father's voice,
we knew what we must do.
We found new friends who, in His
sight, shone very brightly too.

I was there
when He laughed
for joy, to bless the
precious youth.
He loved to teach them
all about His Father's
glorious truth.

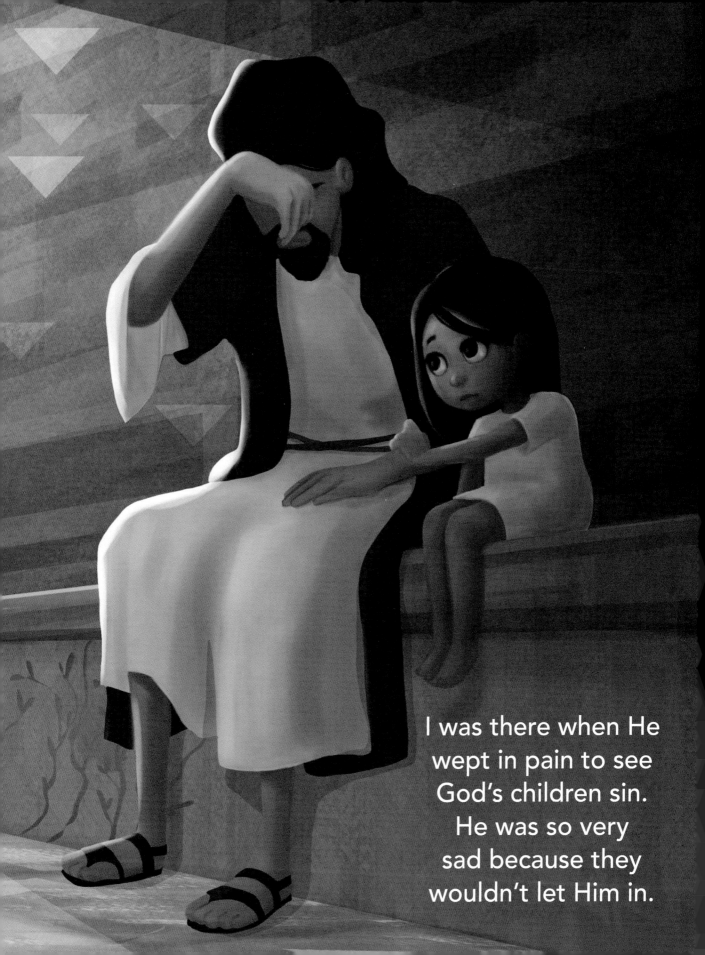

I was there when He
wept in pain to see
God's children sin.
He was so very
sad because they
wouldn't let Him in.

I was there when He calmed the
sky, the tempest of the deep.
Just like those winds, He'll calm
life's storms for His beloved sheep.

And I was with Him when He bled
for every child of God.
His strength to suffer all for us,
it left me very awed.

Even though I couldn't do much,
of course I had to try
to give my comfort unto Him
as He sent His prayers up high.

Then, when He hung upon the
cross, I knew my mission's end.
So I went back up to heaven and
had to leave my Friend.

Up in heaven,
I thought deeply
about all that I had learned.
I'd done my best to serve my
Friend till the day that I returned.

I, the Littlest, with my flaws,
even though I was small.
In the end, my part to
be true was enough
after all.

And when I come to Earth again,
this time all on my own,
I'll recognize my Friend and know
I'll never be alone.

Thou shalt
abide in me, and
I in you;
therefore walk
with me.

Moses 6:34